Knocking the Rice

Story Keeper Series
Book 9

Dave and Pat Sargent (*left*) are longtime residents of Prairie Grove, Arkansas. Dave, a fourth-generation dairy farmer, began writing in early December 1990. Pat, a former teacher, began writing in the fourth grade. They enjoy the outdoors and have a real love for animals.

Sue Rogers (*right*) returned to her beloved Mississippi after retirement. She shared books with children for more than thirty years. These stories fulfill a dream of writing books—to continue the sharing.

Knocking the Rice

Story Keeper Series
Book 9

By Dave and Pat Sargent
and Sue Rogers

Beyond "The End"
By Sue Rogers

Illustrated by Jane Lenoir

Ozark Publishing, Inc.
P.O. Box 228
Prairie Grove, AR 72753

Cataloging-in-Publication Data

Sargent, Dave, 1941–
Knocking the rice / by Dave and Pat Sargent and Sue Rogers ; illustrated by Jane Lenoir.—Prairie Grove, AR : Ozark Publishing, c2004.
p. cm. (Story keeper series ; 9)

"Be powerful"—Cover
SUMMARY: Istas takes us through the four seasons of a Chippewa year—where they live and how they gather the food that sustains them. Her mother, who is very important to her, is in danger. Can Istas save her?
ISBN 1-56763-919-4 (hc)
1-56763-920-8 (pbk)

1. Indians of North America—Juvenile fiction. 2. Chippewa Indians—Juvenile fiction. [1. Native Americans—United States—Fiction. 2. Chippewa Indians—Fiction.] 1. Sargent, Pat, 1936– II. Rogers, Sue, 1933– III. Lenoir, Jane, 1950– ill. IV. Title. V. Series.
PZ7.S243Kn 2004
Fic]—dc21 2003091111

Printed in the United States of America

Inspired by

a people who used the lakes
and rivers of their region
like a vast highway network.

Dedicated to

children who remind me
of what is truly important.

Foreword

Istas, a young Chippewa girl, is learning to do all the things her mother does. The thing she likes to do most is to sing the songs she has learned from her mother. Her family has a different home for each season of the year. In the fall, her mother is lost. No one can find her. What can Istas do to help her mother?

Contents

If you would like to have the authors of the Story Keepers Series visit your school, free of charge, just call us at 1-800-321-5671.

One

Mother

Inside a Chippewa wigwam, deep in a forest beyond the bitter winds of Lake Huron, came the first cry of a baby girl. The mother wrapped her baby in a warm blanket made of rabbit fur and sang a gentle lullaby. She named her daughter Istas. I know, because I am that baby. My name means "snow".

My grandmother made a dream catcher for my cradleboard. It was in the shape of a circle to show how the sun travels across the sky. It had a small hole in the center where good dreams could come through. With the first rays of sunlight, the bad dreams would perish. Grandmother also put an owl feather in the dream catcher—it was a woman's feather, for wisdom.

Grandmother would have used an eagle feather, for courage, if I had been a boy.

Eight winters have passed since that cold night. I have heard my mother sing the lullaby to other babies—my brothers and sisters. I sing it to them sometimes, and watch their sleepy brown eyes close. I sing them other songs I have learned from my mother. The song I like most to hear my mother sing is "Do Not Weep." These song words call us to stop our play and come to our mother. We laugh when we gather around her. She smiles.

My mother keeps her long hair oiled with bear grease. She braids it in a long braid. She arranges it to flatter her face. Her dress is made of deerskins. The moccasins she wears in winter are sewn to her leggings. She embroiders designs on them. It is her songs that make her pretty.

All the clothes for our family are handmade by my mother. Moccasins are made with puffed seams and colored with red, yellow, blue, and green dyes. She also makes pretty jewelry for us.

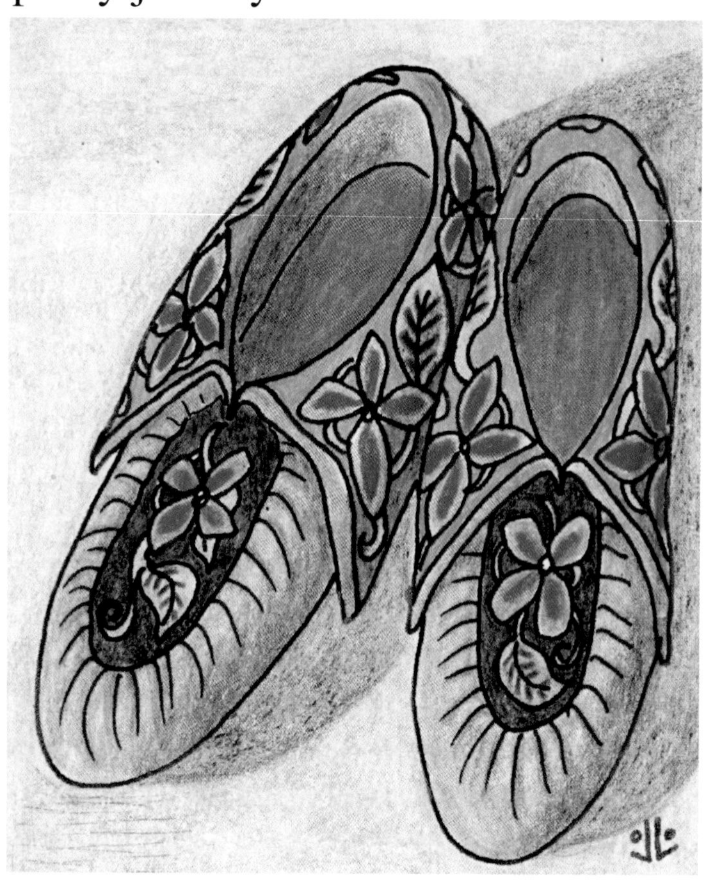

My mother knows where to gather nuts, berries, and wild rice. She cooks good-tasting food. She can cover a wigwam. She hangs a moose hide in the doorway to keep out the winter winds. She covers the ground inside with cedar branches and rush mats. It is snug and warm.

Our beds are like sleeping on air. Mother makes them by covering spruce boughs with animal skins. But it is her songs that make us sleep.

With skilled hands, my mother can split the bark of large birch trees into six to nine layers. I watch her so I can learn. The first thing she taught me was to cut birchbark dolls for my little sisters.

Sometimes my brothers want me to make bundle wrappers for their treasures. Pots for cooking are made from birchbark. Bark is used to make buckets, boxes, trays, bowls, and cups. Food wrapped in birchbark will not spoil. My mother works hard, but her songs keep her happy.

One day my grandmother said, "Come, Istas. Bring a piece of birchbark. We will use it and some turkey feathers to make Big Grand a nice fan. He needs one to make a cool breeze. I will etch it with designs to show that he is a good leader."

Mother provides birchbark for my father's canoes. He keeps four canoes. One for a single person is used for his travel. He sometimes races in this little canoe. That is how he won my warm hood made from a deer's head. A much larger canoe is used when he is trading.

Two canoes are for mother and grandmother when harvesting rice.

Two

Sugaring Time

There are six families at our winter-hunting camp. Father and the other men go deep into the woods to hunt and trap. Father's skills provide most of our food. The women dry the meat and cure the animal hides.

Big Grand keeps records of our family on big sheets of birchbark. He draws pictures to remind us of battles, hunts, hungry winters, births, deaths, and other special happenings. He also puts stories on the bark to tell us how to worship and what sort of life we should live.

One winter, Big Grand carved shapes of animals, moons, and stars into wooden molds.

I asked, “What are you making, Big Grand?”

“Just something for a sweet tooth,” he answered with a smile. He laughed when I put a chip of the carvings in my mouth. Ugh. It did not taste sweet at all.

One day my father said, "One moon after another has gone by. Spring is near. We must get to the sugar bush."

There was a flurry of activity. The women wrapped the dried meat in tanned deerskins. The men packed their furs on sleds or toboggans. They made snowshoes for all who would be walking.

"Here, my little snow girl," said my father. "I made these bear-paw snowshoes just for you."

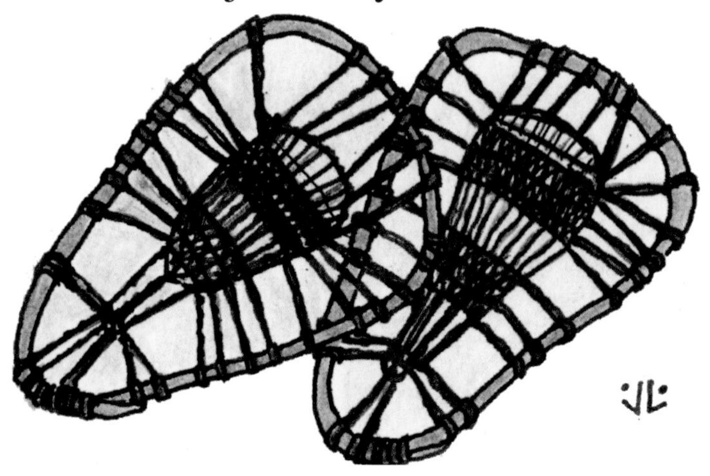

We were off—over, around, and through the snow. It was a happy time. I helped Mother. We sang together.

Mother and the other women talked about the food cache near the sugar camp. They stored all kinds of food there in the fall. There were long strands of dried potatoes and apples, as well as cranberries. There were cedar-bark bags of rice. My grandmother was in charge of the food. She would teach the girls to help and send the boys to the little creeks to catch small fish. The men would cut holes in the ice of the big lakes. They would catch big fish through the ice.

As soon as we got to the sugar bush, the young girls took the birch-bark dishes out of storage. The men repaired the roofs of the huts. The women made fires and began tapping the trees. Then everyone was kept busy all day, running pails of sap to the boilers. The boilers dropped hot rocks into the containers of sap until the water boiled away and nothing

was left but sweet maple sugar.

A large amount of sugar was made. Sugar is a basic seasoning for grains and breads, stews, teas, berries, and vegetables. Maple sugar is used as a preservative in dried food. It is mixed with wild onions for a cough medicine and used for other ailments. Maple sugar is so important to my people, that it gives its name to the moon (month) when sugaring takes place: *Izhkigamisegi Geezis*. This means the moon of boiling.

We found out what Big Grand's molds were for. Mother made soft sugar from some of the maple syrup. Then she pressed it into the molds. When it hardened, we had a sweet surprise—maple candy!

"Oh, thank you, Big Grand.

Thank you, Mother," I cried. "Maple candy is even better than dripping maple syrup over scoops of snow!" I sang a song to show Mother how

much I loved her.

When there was enough maple sugar, we headed back to our summer village on the shores of Lake Huron. We sang this song as we looked forward to the warmth and fullness of summer:

"As my eyes search the prairie
I feel the summer in the spring."

Three

Manoominike Giizis

Mahnomin (wild rice) is the basic food for my people. It gives its name to the moon when it is harvested, Manoominike Giizis. In late summer when the rice is ripe, our kin family camps by the marshes where it grows.

Ricing is done in canoes. My mother sits in the stern of her canoe. It takes a strong man using a long pole to push her canoe through the thick rice reeds.

Mother has two long sticks called knockers. She goes through the rice field sweeping one knocker over a bunch of rice reeds, bending them into the canoe, and hitting the heads sharply with the other knocker. The ripest grains fall into the canoe.

After the ripe grains fall into the canoe, my mother lets the reeds spring back up. She never takes all the rice. Some must be left to reseed and some for the birds.

The filled canoe is poled back to the camp. The rice is spread to dry, parched, winnowed, and stored for year-round use.

One day all the canoes were back except my mother's. She was fast at knocking the rice. Her canoe was usually one of the first to fill. Why was she not back? The sun was still in the sky. "She will be back soon," I told myself. But she was not. I ran to tell Big Grand. He sent two of the young men out to look for her. The sun sank. It became dark. The two men returned. They had not found Mother's canoe.

"Come inside, Little Snow," said Big Grand. "We will look for your mother again when the sun gives light."

"Please, Big Grand, let me stay here," I said.

"You may stay, Little Snow. You will be safe," he said. "I will bring a blanket."

A hush settled over the camp. Everyone was sleeping. The ache in my heart would not let me sleep. Where was my mother?

In the shadows, I saw a man climb out of the water. He lay down on the grass. I ran to him. It was the man who had polled mother's canoe!

"Where is my mother?" I cried.

I could barely hear his weak answer, "My pole snapped in two. It knocked me out of the canoe. The force shot the canoe like an arrow. I looked and looked for the canoe but could not find it. I called to your mother, but she did not answer. I have been swimming in the cold water ever since." Then he was asleep. I could not wake him.

I called Big Grand and ran back to the edge of the lake. I began to sing the song my mother sang to call us to her. I sang louder and louder. Big Grand and others came to take care of the young man. They built a big fire. The brighter the fire burned, the louder I sang! I sang on and on.

Big Grand put his hand on my shoulder. He motioned for me to be still and listen. We listened. Out of the darkness came my mother's beautiful voice! Soon she was safe inside our wigwam.

My mother said that when the canoe shot away, she bumped her head and was knocked out. The sun was gone when she came to. She could not find the young man, but part of the pole was on top of the rice. She managed to move the canoe, but did not know which way to go. She was ready to give up until the sun came up. And then, she heard me singing. She followed my voice. Now she is home!

The songs of my people are sung for celebrations, prayers, and for thanksgiving. When I first sang "Do Not Weep," I sang it for prayers. I sing it now for thanksgiving.

Four

Chippewa Facts

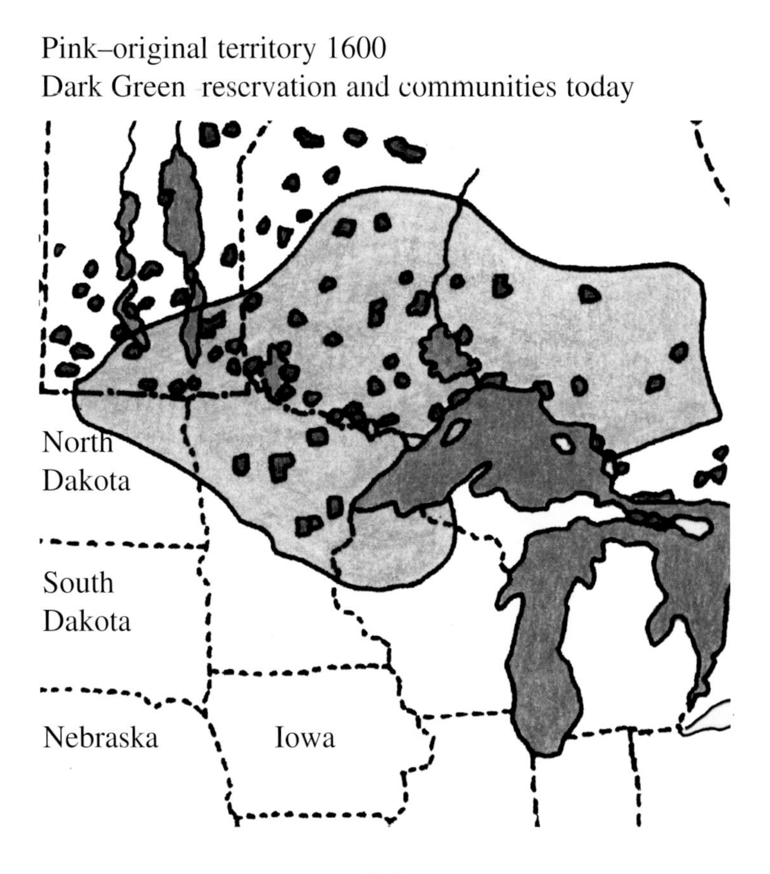

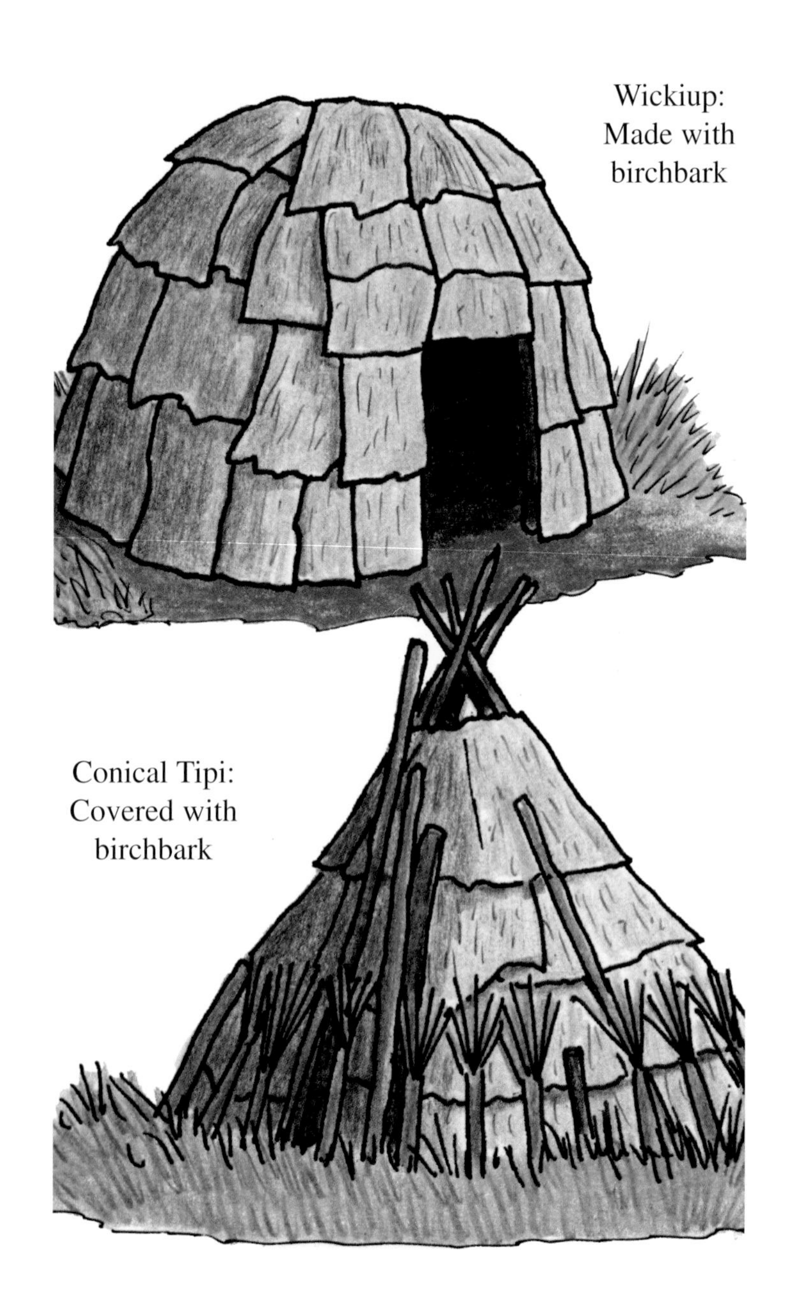
Wickiup:
Made with
birchbark
Conical Tipi:
Covered with
birchbark

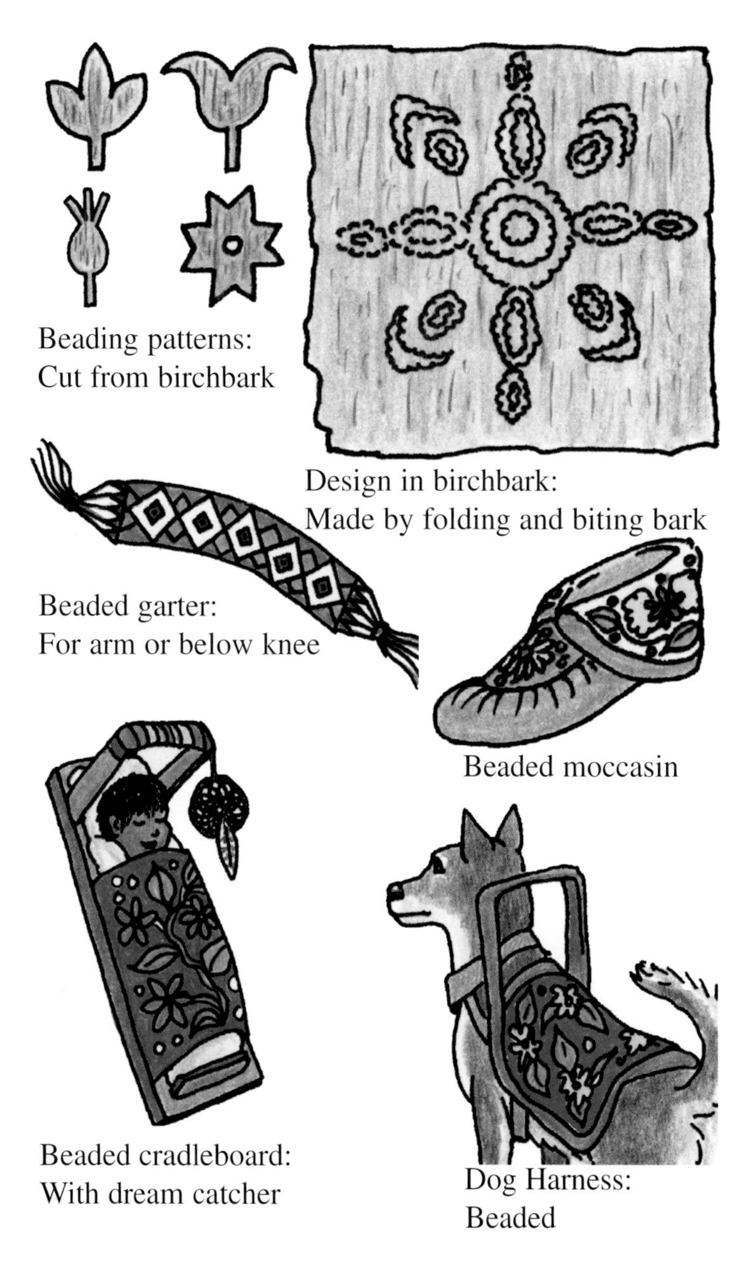

Beading patterns:
Cut from birchbark

Design in birchbark:
Made by folding and biting bark

Beaded garter:
For arm or below knee

Beaded moccasin

Beaded cradleboard:
With dream catcher

Dog Harness:
Beaded

Leather shirt:
Beaded, fringed with
hair and tin cones
Bandolier bag:
(medicine bag)

Newer Type Shirt: Beaded

Leather shirt:
With underdress of plant
fiber (work clothing)

Bear paw snowshoe:
good in underbrush

Ojibwa-type snowshoe:
For long trips and
open ground

Gathering maple syrup in birchbark containers

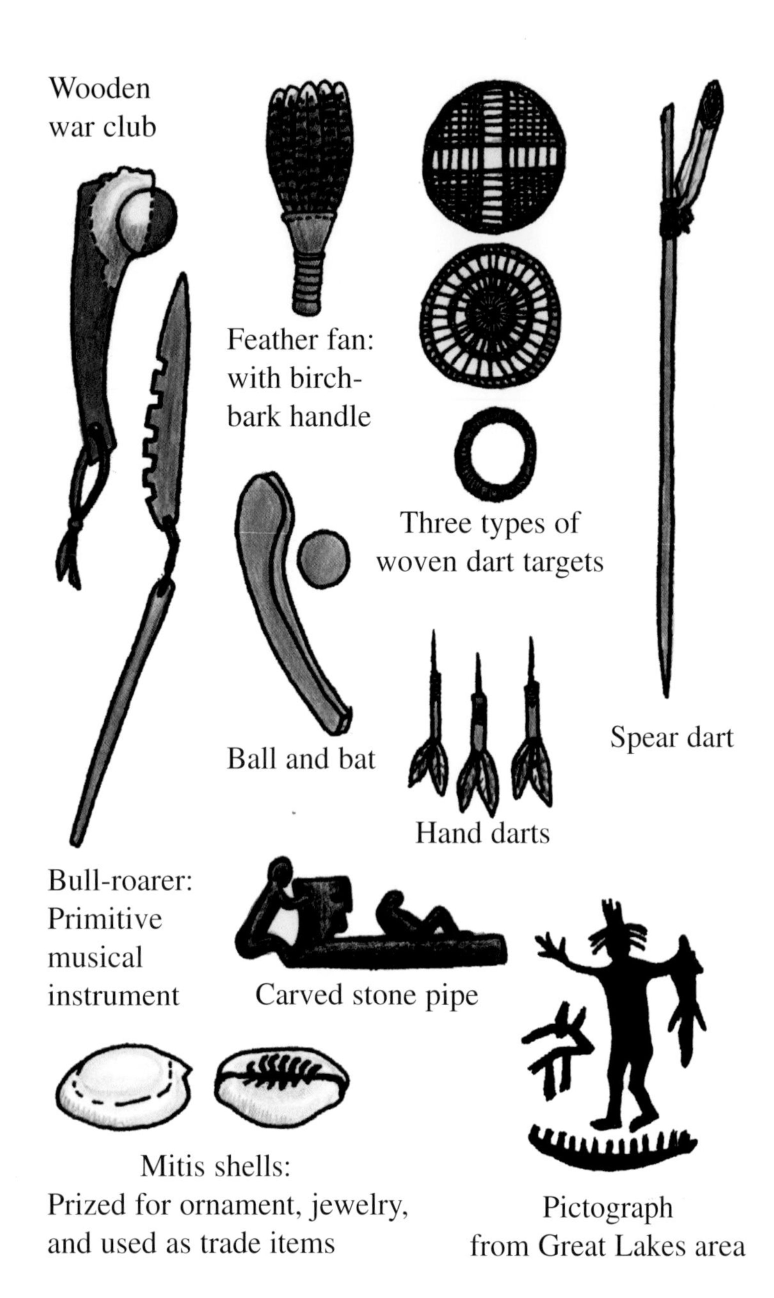
Wooden
war club
Feather fan:
with birch-
bark handle
Three types of
woven dart targets
Ball and bat
Spear dart
Hand darts
Bull-roarer:
Primitive
musical
instrument
Carved stone pipe
Mitis shells:
Prized for ornament, jewelry,
and used as trade items
Pictograph
from Great Lakes area

Beyond "The End"

LANGUAGE LINKS

● It takes a group of words to make an interesting story. Some words in this story are very interesting, such as:

1. You know what cash is, but what is a *cache*?
2. How do you *pole* a canoe?
3. What would you do to *winnow* the rice?
4. Draw a *puffed seam* moccasin.
5. What does *etch* mean?
6. Describe a *flurry*.
7. Watch a friend's mouth when he or she says *wigwam*.

Be on the lookout for new words!

CURRICULUM CONNECTIONS

● Check the weather! Istas and her family might have lived near what is now Sault Ste. Marie, Michigan. Her relatives may still live there. Locate this city on a map. Go to this website <www.nws.noaa.gov/forecasts.html>. This is the National Weather Service. In the search box in the left column on your screen (not the one on top) type *Sault Ste. Marie, MI* (You must use the period.). Click "Go."

1. How cold is it there today?
2. What is the forecast for tomorrow?
3. What is the forecast for Sunday?
4. How deep is the snow now? (Scroll down to box *Snowdepth Map* to see.)
5. What would you wear there?

● Istas made some birchbark bundle wrappers for the treasures her little brothers collected. What do you think would have been a treasure to a Chippewa boy?

● Chippewa people built their homes with materials from trees. So do we. How does the lumber in our homes differ from the tree products in Istas' home? How do you tell the age of a tree?

● Remember when Istas talked about "dripping maple syrup over scoops of snow"? That treat today is called *Sugar-on-Snow* or *Leather Aprons*. Istas had plenty of snow. You might want to use shaved ice. See a recipe at website <www. massmaple.org/sos.html>. WATCH OUT! Ask an adult to make this for you. The syrup is **very** hot!

- Big Grand needed a new fan. Istas and her grandmother made one for him. You can make a fan for your grandfather. See information and instructions at the following website: <www.nativetech.org/brchbark/barkfan.html>.
- Here are two websites your music teacher might like. The song Istas sang for her mother, "Do Not Weep," is in the first site: <www.inquiry.net/outdoor/native/song/index.htm>. This website tells that the Chippewa have always been fond of singing: <www.pbs.org/riverofsong/music/e1-ojibway.html>. (Note: the 1 part of the address e1 is the number 1, not the letter l.) This is a part of a unit on the Mississippi River.

● You looked at the weather forecast on the National Weather Service home page for Sault Ste. Marie, MI. What are other sources for information about the weather? Make a list. Don't forget to list the radio and newspaper. Ask your librarian to show you an atlas that tells about the weather in different countries. Do you have a local phone number that gives *time-temperature-weather*? Your list is growing! Keep listing!

● Chippewa storytellers tell how to this day Spider Woman builds her lodge before dawn. If you look at it before dawn, you will see the miracle of how she captures the sunrise as the light sparkles on the dew gathered there. You will see a small hole in the center. It lets the good dreams you had in the night come through. With the first rays of sunlight, the bad dreams are destroyed.

This summer, try to find a spiderweb before the sun. Watch the sparkles the sun makes. Marvel at how the tiny spider makes such a beautiful thing. Try to think of something you can do to make someone you love happy.